Dommy B has won many awards, including the Saboteur Award for the UK's Best Spoken Word Performer (twice!). He has been Glastonbury Festival's poet-in-residence and appeared on BBC's *Rhyme Rocket*.

Each of his exciting tales for children have been adapted from his acclaimed poetry theatre shows.

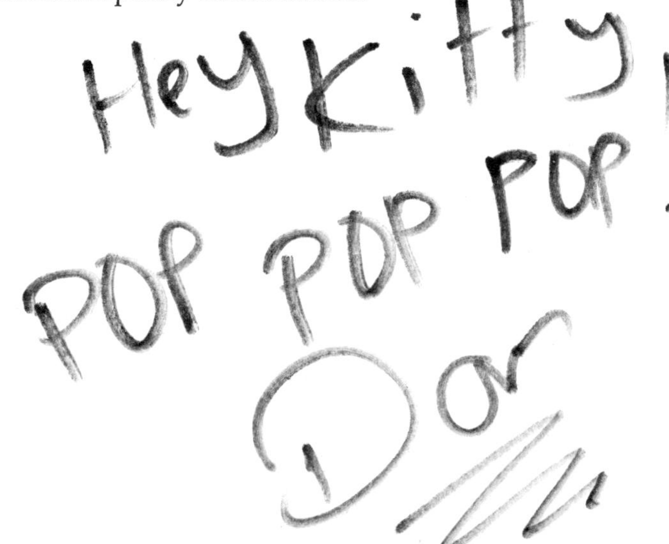

*By the author*

Spark, the Goblin Wizard

When Trolls Try to Eat Your Goldfish

The Dragon Who Hates Poetry

Aaaaaaaaaaaaagh! Dinosaurs!

Best Adventure Ever!

# THE STORY OF DOMMY B'S

# BEST ADVENTURE EVER!

Flapjack Press
flapjackpress.co.uk

Exploring the synergy between performance and the page

Published in 2021 by Flapjack Press
Salford, Gtr Manchester
flapjackpress.co.uk



ISBN 978-0-9576639-4-7

Illustrations & cover design by Brink
paulneads.co.uk

Cover photograph: Scott Dawson
Page 1 photograph: Z-arts
Courtesy of the author

Printed by Imprint Digital
Exeter, Devon
digital.imprint.co.uk

Theatrical production developed with funding from

*Dedicated to Michelle.*

*Your enthusiasm, creativity, compassion*
*and spark are wonderful.*
*You give so much to so many*
*and always share fun.*
*I have had no better adventure*
*than my friendship with you!*

## Contents

## Chapter One

## The Story of 'Moving'

When I was ten years old, Mum said we had to move, to live closer to Auntie Lisa, and that meant I would have to go to a new school.

It was late and dark on a Sunday evening when we arrived at our new home, just two doors down from Auntie Lisa's.

I remember my first night in my new home, lying awake in a new bed, too nervous to get to sleep because the next day would be my first day at the new school.

I remember how much I was missing my old friends, now that Mum and me had moved so far away.

“I only have one dream tonight.
I wish I could go back.
I didn't want to move away,
so I will not unpack.
I'll just ignore this box of clothes.
Instead, I'll lie in bed.
I'll look at all the memories
I've kept inside my head.

I'll close my eyes to see my friends,
remember games we played.
We never had the latest toys,
but with our hands we made
a first-place trophy out of stickers and
an empty jar.
My room became a racing track.
This box became a car.

And we'd pretend that we were racing,
all my friends and me.
Inside this box!
There's nowhere else that I would rather be.
But now I've moved, my clothes fill up
this box we used for fun.
I want to see my friends again.
The games we played aren't done.”

For my first day of school, Mum walked me there.

We played a game as we went. Every time we saw a magpie, we both had to hop on one leg three times.

We hopped past a massive park on our right. On our left was the High School, the school for the big kids, where a group of teenagers stood watching as we hopped. We passed them by and crossed over the road to my school's gates.

Mum gave me a big hug and said she was sure I would soon make new friends.

## Chapter Two

## New Day, New School

In class, the teacher made me stand in front of everyone.

"Well," she said, "this is Dom's first day. Who'd like him to sit next to them?"

I will tell you who put their hand up. No one.

Miss told me to sit next to the only boy who was sitting at a desk on his own.

Connor.

Connor had a long fringe which completely covered his eyes – like a yeti. He smiled a lot, but not in a happy way.

He smiled like adults do when they see someone they know in the street and they do not want to say 'hello', but they also do not want to *not* say 'hello' because they do not want to be rude, so they give an awkward flat smile which means 'please don't talk to me'.

That was Connor's standard look.

When Miss asked questions, other children answered, but Connor did not speak until the bell rang for morning break.

That was when Connor finally said, "Ummm, Dom, if you wanted, would you like to play a really cool game?"

Connor led me through the playground, away from the other kids, to a narrow alley between the nursery block and the old brick wall which went around the school.

In this alley, Connor and his brother from the year below took turns to be a little, happy *bunny*.

The other was a *zombie bunny*!

Their game was that the happy bunny had to hop through the alley without getting caught by the zombie.

I watched them for a little bit and then said, "You know what? I can make this game even better. You two both be zombies, but be quick. Make it difficult. I can leg it past you, and then—"

"That's not how we play," interrupted Connor's little brother. "You don't know the rules."

I shook my head.

"Well, I don't need to know 'rules'. I know everything there is to know about zombies… and every kind of monster. I'm a monster expert! You know, at my old school, I once met a real goblin."

I started to tell Connor and his brother an epic rhyme about the time when I actually *did* meet a goblin.

## Chapter Three

## The Story of 'Three Wishes'

"When a goblin burst from a
bright white light,
right in my way,
she said, *"Hey!*
*I will make three wishes come true*
*for you."*

Wow! Three wishes?
I could make myself invisible,
or I could make myself the best at football,
or I could wish for one million chocolate cakes
and then eat them all!
Or... I could make the world better.
My wish could create peace on Earth forever.

I said, *"Goblin, please,*
*I would love to live in a world where there was only*
*peace."*

The goblin grinned.
She stroked her chin.
*"I can do that.*
*Magic! Begin!"*

***Zap!***

Maybe that goblin misheard me when I spoke,
or maybe she was playing a very cruel joke,
but her magic did not make a world where there was only peace.
Her magic made a world where there was only
peas...

Mushy peas.

Houses, shops
and office blocks
all turned to mushy peas.
Parks full of trees became
mushy peas.
People turned to mushy peas
right before my eyes.
Mushy pea birds
fell from mushy pea skies.
*Splat!*

I looked at
the mushy pea street.
Mushy pea ground beneath my mushy pea feet.
I saw my hands turn green
and started to scream,

*"This is obscene!*
*I'm turning into mushy peas!*
*Goblin, please! Make everything normal.*
*It is unacceptable*
*to turn the world into*
*a vegetable."*

The goblin grinned.
She started to chortle.
*"Is that your second wish?*
*Make everything… 'normal'?"*

**Zap!!**

I looked around
and found
my hands were back to normal. I mean,
not green!

Phew! I ran home to Mum. I said,
*"Mum! You wanna play?"*
…and she answered in a normal voice,
*"No, Dominic. Not today…"*

…What? Mum *never* called me Dominic.
She would call me a weird name
like *"Domsta Monster!"*,
and then we'd always play a game
like *"Can we find a dragon
in the park today?"*,
but now Mum was all formal
and she didn't want to play.

Then things got much worse, *much* worse,
much worse than I'd first feared.
My second wish had made *everyone* normal.
*Nobody* was weird.

OK. You might think,
*"Why would that be bad?"*
Isn't it good to be normal?
Wouldn't that make people glad?

But… with *everyone* in a
normal state,
everyone was fine,
but no one was great.

There were no crazy artists,
no amazing mathematicians,
no hilarious YouTube stars,
no nuclear physicians,
no video game makers,
no Premier League footballers!

Across the whole world, people were all just the same as each other.
No one stood out.
Everyone normal. Normal. *Normal!*

I had no doubt
exactly how to make my last wish.

*"Oi! Goblin, listen to this.*
*Whatever I wish for, the worse the world gets.*
*My last wish…*
*I wish you and I never met."*

The goblin grinned.
She clicked her claws.
*"Fine!*
*I'll make the world just as it was."*

# Zap!!!

And with that she was gone.
My third wish was done…

and I had back
my silly Mum!

She said, *"Hey, Domsta Monsta!*
*Don't get left behind!*
*Let's go to the park,*
*there are dragons we must find!"*

And here is my point – that goblin deceived me.
I tell you, it's true, though you might not believe me.
All proof of that goblin has now disappeared.
You might say believing all that makes me… 'weird',

but 'weird' is not an insult.
It's a compliment to me.
I've seen how *sad* a world
without weird people would be. ”

## Chapter Four

## Games

When I finished the last line of my magic goblin rhyme, I hoped that Connor and his little brother would be impressed.

But when I looked back over to see their reaction, they did not seem impressed. They did not even seem like they had been listening. In fact, the two of them had gone back to playing zombie bunnies again, without me.

I could not believe it. I had just told them about my best adventure ever and they had not even listened!

So, when we were back in class, *I* ignored Connor all through the next lesson to see how he liked it! (Although I do not know if he even noticed, because he was not speaking to anyone anyway.)

Whilst I was ignoring Connor, I noticed one of the other boys in my class whispering to the girl he was sitting next to.

I heard him say: "Aisha! Gimme a target."

I heard her say: "OK. There."

Then this boy flicked a rubber band all the way to the back of the class!

THWANNNG!

Miss did not see what he had done, but some of the other kids did and they started sniggering. I started sniggering!

I wished I was sitting with Rubber Band Boy, a kid who seemed fun, instead of Connor, a kid who hardly ever spoke.

At dinner break, I ran into the playground, up to Rubber Band Boy and Aisha.

Rubber Band Boy was holding a muddy football. Aisha had a big toy kitten in one of her pockets, just its head popping out. This kitten had a silver ring pierced through one ear.

I told Aisha and Rubber Band Boy I was going to tell them my goblin rhyme…

> "When a goblin burst from a
> bright white light,
> right in my way,
> she said, *"Hey!*
> *I will make three wishes— "*

"Hold on, hold on, hold on," said Aisha. "Why are you doing that weird voice?"

I hesitated.

"Well… That's a goblin voice… isn't it?"

Aisha looked uncertain.

"Why would you want to make yourself sound weird?"

"Well… it's good to be weird. Being different is interesting. Yeah?"

Aisha raised her eyebrows.

"No. In this school, if you are weird, no one will want to be your friend. Do you want to have no friends? Nah, I'm not listening to this. Come on, Jack. Let's go."

Rubber Band Boy, whose name it seemed was Jack, said nothing. He and Aisha walked away and joined some of the others to play football.

I had thought everyone at this new school would have loved my rhymes, but so far nothing was going the way I had hoped it would.

All that day, Jack and Aisha stayed together. I sat by myself and watched them as they laughed and played games.

I wondered, what would Jack have thought of my goblin rhyme if Aisha had not been there?

☆ ☆ ☆

At home time, Mum met me at the school gates and asked how my first day had been, so I told her everything.

"Domsta Monsta," she said, "it was just your first day. Things will get better, I promise."

Then we saw a magpie, so we both hopped on one leg three times. Mum always knew how to cheer me up.

That night, I went to sleep in my new room confident Mum was right.

Everything would get better.

**AISHA** **#10/52**

| **Height:** 139cm | **Eyes:** Brown |
| --- | --- |
| **Favourite Food:** Brussel sprouts and pizza (not combined). | |
| **Top Speed:** 100% (including leaping tall obstacles on any bicycle). | |
| **Unique Skills:** 100% (excels in football with unmatched ability in goal, defence, midfield and attack). | |
| **Creativity:** 100% (can mimic wide range of sounds for comedic and stealth value). | |
| **Power Up:** Combine with 'Pierced-ear Toy Kitten' card #41. This lucky charm boosts confidence. Auto-win on Unique Skills. | |

## Chapter Five

## What I Did on the Worst Morning Ever

The next morning, when Mum was getting my breakfast, she fell.

She did not trip. She just suddenly fell.

She hit the back of her head on the hard kitchen floor and she did not get back up.

"Mum? What's wrong? Mum? Wake up!"

No response.

What could I do? I could not go out to ask Auntie Lisa for help because I did not want to leave Mum on her own. Full of fear, I picked up the phone.

"Hello… Ambulance please. My Mum's not moving."

Eventually, two paramedics turned up. One knelt down by Mum whilst the other led me outside and knocked on the door of Auntie Lisa's house.

Auntie Lisa gave me a hug. She and I watched as the paramedics carried Mum on a stretcher into the ambulance and took her away.

Auntie Lisa went in to make me a packed lunch.

I sat on my own in her garden by the flower beds. I looked at the marigolds, geraniums and roses, and wondered if I could bring a bunch of flowers for Mum in hospital.

Auntie Lisa said she would rather I did not touch anything in her garden. As she drove me to school, she said that once Mum was well enough for visitors we could buy her something from the florist.

By the time Auntie Lisa dropped me off it was already morning break.

In the playground, a big group was gathered around Rubber Band Boy.

Jack was doing strange moves. He was leaping and striking the air with his fists and his feet. He was telling everyone that his big brother had taught him how to be a ninja.

Connor was not there, but everyone else from class was listening. Aisha was at the front of the crowd with her toy kitten, hugging it as Jack spoke.

"OK. If you wanna learn ninja moves, I can teach you. Me, I can defend myself from anyone. Even the kids from the High School. Did you hear about the High School gang who got a kid from Year 3, tied him up in a bin bag and threw him in a skip? He came out covered in dog food from half empty tins people had chucked away. He stunk so bad dogs followed him, trying to sniff him, for a week. If anyone tried to do that to me, I'd get those dog food tins and make *them* eat dog food. Do you know what happens if you eat dog food? Gives you hairy hands. Ha!"

Everyone laughed at Jack's story.

Everyone was impressed.

## Chapter Six

## What Jack Gave Me

I went inside and told Miss what had happened with Mum.

Miss was really kind. She listened. She said I could talk to her any time I needed.

Then, in our afternoon class, I heard:

"Pssst…! …Pssst!"

From the desk next to mine, Jack was holding out a little piece of paper to me.

On the paper was a drawing of Connor.

Connor had a dozen rubber bands all being fired at his bum. His bum was exploding! Bits of bum everywhere!

I tried not to laugh, but Miss saw me with the paper and started to walk towards my desk. I stuffed the paper as quickly as I could into my trouser pocket.

"Dominic, show me what you put in your pocket."

"I can't, Miss."

"Why not?"

"It's... it's a tissue. I can't get it out. It's covered in snot."

The whole class laughed. Jack laughed. It felt great to make everyone laugh.

Miss was about to say something... when the bell rang for home time. As everyone was bustling out of their seats to get coats and bags, Miss raised her voice above the noise.

"Don't forget, tomorrow is our class trip to the park. Don't run, Jack! Thank you. Dominic, may I speak with you, please. Yes, goodbye, Aisha..."

When everyone else was gone, Miss sat down beside me. She looked disappointed.

"Dominic, I know it's a difficult time with what's happened with your Mum, but that doesn't mean you can be cheeky, does it?"

"I wasn't being cheeky, Miss. I really do have a snotty tissue. I can show you."

"No. That's OK. Look. Don't forget tomorrow is our trip to the park. OK? Best behaviour please."

I ran out of class, across the playground, hoping I would catch Jack. But he was gone.

The only kid still there was Connor.

"Hey, Dom! If you wanted, would you like to walk together?"

Connor had a bike, but did not get on. He walked, holding his bike by his side.

Now, I had not forgotten how Connor ignored my goblin rhyme, so he was not my favourite person, but I thought, what harm would it do to just let him follow?

Connor said he was sorry to hear what had happened with Mum. He said if I needed to know anything about any of the kids in class, he could tell me.

When we got near the High School, we saw a teenager leaning against a wall and Connor suddenly stopped.

"Oh, Dom! That's Jack's big brother. Did you hear what he did to that Year 3 kid? Tied him in a bin bag and threw him in a skip. I'm not staying here. See you tomorrow. Bye."

With that, Connor jumped onto his bike and cycled away.

I looked back at Jack's big brother. He had not been looking at us. Why would he have any reason to hurt me?

I started to walk in front of him and… he did not even look up. I knew I had nothing to worry about! I confidently headed on to Auntie Lisa's, hoping there might be news about Mum, hoping that Mum might soon be better and back home with me.

## CONNOR #33/52

| **Height:** 139cm | **Eyes:** Brown |
|---|---|
| **Favourite Food:** Apples and chippy chips (not combined). | |
| **Top Speed:** 100% (aided by constant bicycle maintenance and perfect highway safety awareness). | |
| **Unique Skills:** 100% (mathematical expert, unshakeable photographic memory of all other cards). | |
| **Creativity:** 100% (exemplary imaginative prowess in written and physical games). | |
| **Power Up:** Combine with 'Younger Brother' card #47. Brilliant bunny hops and patience learned from living with an annoying sibling. Auto-win on Creativity. | |

## Chapter Seven

## The Story of 'Jackiddy Jack'

Auntie Lisa said she had spoken to the hospital. She said we could not visit Mum just yet. She tried to look calm, but I could not help think that did not sound good.

I lay on the bed in Auntie Lisa's spare room and looked at the drawing Jack had given me.

Jack could have given this to anyone. Out of everyone in class, he gave this drawing to *me*.

I decided I would thank Jack for this drawing by making up a new rhyme all about him.

Excitedly, I started to write…

"Jackiddy Jack
can attack
in your back
with a whack!
Jackiddy Jack!
Jackiddy Jack!

Jack has all the super skills
the other kids lack.
He wears a ninja belt.
It's a belt which is black.
His kicks are so quick.
He can make a brick crack.
His teeth are so strong.
He eats rocks for a snack!

He's clever with computers.
There is nothing he can't hack.
He's brilliant telling jokes.
He always has a wisecrack.
He won't get lost.
Without a compass, he'll find any track,
'cos Jack is awesome! He's the best!
The leader of the pack!

Jackiddy Jack
can attack
in your back
with a whack!
Jackiddy Jack!
Jackiddy Jack!"

I lay in bed very happy with the rhyme I had made. I could not wait to show Jack!

My last thought before I fell asleep was that if a goblin gave me three wishes now, my first wish would be to be as cool as Jack.

If I could be as cool as Jack, maybe we would be best friends.

Then I would wish Mum was well again.

Then I would wish for a big party. Mum, Jack, and all my friends from my old school.

Together.

## Chapter Eight

## A Trip to the Park

Wednesday morning, Auntie Lisa let me walk to school, where I saw my new friend.

"Hey! Jack! Jackiddy Jack!"

He was on the other side of the playground, so must not have heard me.

I saw he had a big bruise on his face, like he had been in a fight. It looked painful.

*Wow.* I thought, if Jack has a black eye, I would hate to see the state of the other guy.

At the park, something brilliant happened.

Miss partnered Connor with Aisha, and put *me* with *Jack!*

I asked if his eye was hurting, but Jack said it was nothing. I wondered whether now was a good time to show him the rhyme I had written. No. I decided after school would be better. I decided that at home time, I would ask Jack if he wanted dinner with me at Auntie Lisa's, and I could read him my rhyme there, *really* far away from teachers and the other kids. Especially Aisha. I did not want her to ruin it.

Miss led us to the park's playground. I thought Jack might think swings were a bit babyish, but he loved them. He kept daring me to go higher and higher and higher, and I did. Jack was on the swing next to mine, and I swear two people have never swung as high as we did.

I felt like a ninja.

When it was time for dinner, Miss took us to some wooden tables.

Before I had even opened my packed lunch, Aisha came over, hugging her toy kitten, grinning.

"Hey, Jack. Remember when we came here last year and I did those wicked stunts on my bike, jumping over broken branches by the lake?"

Jack started grinning too.

"Ah, yeah, Aisha, that was sick!"

I joined in.

"I would have loved that. I wish I had a bike, 'cos I can do stunts. I am… 'sick'."

Jack turned to face me. He had a mischievous glint in his eye.

"Is that so, Dom? Hey! You know what? Connor goes to Maths Club after school today. You could borrow his bike, bring it here, without him knowing it was gone, and show Aisha and me your best stunts. Go on. I dare you."

A dare? The truth was I had never actually had a bike of my own, but simple bike stunts could not be that difficult, could they?

"OK," I said, nodding. "I'll ask Connor if I can borrow his bike.

Jack sighed.

"Why ask? Just take it. He won't be using it at Maths Club, will he?"

Aisha turned her back on me.

"This is pointless," she said to Jack. "Dom won't take Connor's bike. He's chicken."

I glared at Aisha. Jack and I had had such a great time on the swings without her and I was not going to let her call me a chicken.

"No no no!" I protested. "I will do it. I can get Connor's bike. No problem."

I did not want her to ruin the chance of Jack and me becoming best friends.

**JACK** **#18/52**

| **Height:** 139cm | **Eyes:** Brown |
|---|---|
| **Favourite Food:** Ketchup sandwiches and bananas (not combined). | |
| **Top Speed:** 100% (with lightning reflexes for head-height air-kicks whilst standing or leaping). | |
| **Unique Skills:** 100% (rubber band slingshots of unparalleled distance). | |
| **Creativity:** 100% (cartoon comic drawing, superb visual joke telling). | |
| **Power Up:** Combine with 'Daily Practice' card #6. Sensational attention to detail. Auto-win on Top Speed. | |

## Chapter Nine

## A Trip at the Park

After school that day, Connor did go to Maths Club, just like Jack said he would.

I hid behind the nursery block until everyone else was gone. Then I crawled along the tarmac and under the Maths Club's window to Connor's bike. I saw his bicycle helmet hanging on one of the handlebars.

I hesitated.

Mum always told me that stealing was bad.

But she also said it was good to share… so it was good for Connor to share his bike. Also, if Mum knew how I was making new friends, she would be happy. That is what Mum wanted.

So, I put on the helmet, jumped on the bike, and excitedly sped out of the school gates.

It felt fantastic, speeding down the road. Riding a bike was easy!

I got to the park.

There was Jack, there was Aisha, and there were some broken tree branches laid out along the path beside the big, park lake.

Jack clapped his hands together.

"OK, Dom," he said. "Show us your stunts."

"He's not going to do it," said Aisha with a mocking, fake laugh. "He's a baby."

"Shut up, Aisha," I said through gritted teeth. "I said I'll do it."

With more than one wobble and a lump in my throat, I cycled to the far end of the path by the lake and then turned back to face the broken branches.

I took a big breath and started forwards.

Picking up speed, my legs pumped the pedals like pistons.

I was nearing the first branch, about to try to jump it, when something sharp stung my ear.

*Ow!* I teetered. Fell. *Splash!* Into the lake! Ice cold! Swirls of water filled my freezing ears.

I pulled myself up, soaked to the skin, to see Jack and Aisha laughing. Aisha had a camera pointed at me.

I put my hand to my trouser pocket. Inside, the paper I had used to write the rhyme for Jack was soggy. It was ruined, and Jack had never even seen it.

Floating in the water, I saw what had hit my ear.

A rubber band.

Jack walked up to me and put his hands on my shoulders. He smiled and pushed me back into the lake.

I felt like a baby.

I got up again, clothes heavy with water, expecting another push, to see Jack holding Connor's bike with both hands.

"This bike is rubbish."

Jack hurled Connor's bike into the lake. *Crack!* That did not sound good.

Then Jack came right up close to me again.

"Dom," he said, "you were... funny. Well done, mate."

I smiled nervously, not sure if I was going to get another push.

"Oh no!" cried Aisha, suddenly. "I've dropped my kitten. She must have fallen out my pocket. She might be in the road. Come on, Jack, we've got to find her."

Jack turned to face Aisha. He was not smiling now.

"Are you joking? I'm not looking for some stupid toy."

Aisha looked surprised.

"Stop messing around. Help me."

"No. If you want to go, go. I'm fine here."

"But, Jack? Jack!"

Aisha gave me a terrible look and then she marched out of the park.

"Umm..." I said, "should we get the bike out the lake now? Maths Club will be over soon."

Jack started walking towards the park gate.

"Later," he said. "You need to change those wet clothes. Let's go back to yours."

So we did. I took off the bike helmet and walked up my street, cold and wet, but happy that Jack was walking with me.

Jack had told me I was funny. We had shared a joke.

The coolest kid in school was now my friend.

## Chapter Ten

## Bang!

Back at Auntie Lisa's, I hurried in quietly, without letting her see. I would not want her to tell Mum I had been doing stuff in the lake and getting in a mess, would I?

Had to stay quiet…

BANG! BANG! BANG!

"Come on, mate! Hurry up!"

"Shhhh! Jack!"

Still pulling on my dry jumper, I rushed back outside.

Jack was in Auntie Lisa's garden holding a fistful of geraniums.

"Jack? What have you done?"

Instead of answering, Jack knelt down on the grass and with both hands ripped up some marigolds. He threw them across the lawn.

"It's a test. Show me you can pull up those roses, without cutting your hand on the thorns. Do that and you'll prove you're a ninja."

"But what about Auntie Lisa…?"

"What about her?" shrugged Jack. "You do know what it means to be a ninja, don't you? Ninjas are always there for each other. Can you imagine that? Never being scared, never being lonely, and always having great adventures, because you're a ninja, like me? Don't you think that sounds good?"

It did sound good. This sounded even better than best friends.

Jack pointed to the flower bed.

"Then prove you are a ninja. Pull up those roses."

I looked down to where Jack was pointing.

"OK… but what about Auntie Lisa?"

Jack kicked the ground hard and a clump of grass flew into the air.

"It doesn't matter! Forget her... and forget your Mum. All adults do is tell you off for having fun and we don't need them. Do we?"

"Jack. Mum's in hospital."

"Is she? No offence, but she sounds weak. Ninjas *never* get hurt."

I looked down to the ground and bit my lip.

"Oh... if that's true Jack, how did you get a black eye?"

"I told you, that's nothing. You should see what I did to other guy."

That is exactly what I had thought when I first noticed Jack's bruise, but now I thought about it, the only time I had actually seen Jack do anything like being a ninja was jumping around in the playground. How did I know any of this was true?

"Well," I said, taking a deep breath, "you should see what *my Mum* did to the other guy. That's why Mum's in hospital, because she... won a fight. She only broke her arm. The other guy is in a full body cast, head to toe!"

Jack said nothing, he just looked me right in the eyes.

"That's not true," he said. "Liar."

"It is true!"

I took a step closer to Jack.

"My Mum is tougher than… a dragon's fire.
If you can lift a heavy weight, my Mum can lift it higher.
She can leap a six-foot fence made out of sharp barbed wire.
Watch her run a marathon. You'll never see her tire.
You couldn't beat her in a fight. She's who I most admire.
I dare you, Jack. You face my Mum. You'll see I'm not a liar."

Jack took a step closer to me.

I tried to not look scared. The truth was I was frightened.

He looked to the upstairs window of Auntie Lisa's, then back at me.

"Nah," he said. "I was going anyway. This place is rubbish. You should have done what I said, little mummy's boy. Big mistake. Your Mum won't be with you in school tomorrow, will she? Tomorrow, when you are all on your own, that's when I'm gonna get you."

With that, Jack ran away.

He was right. Mum did not fight. I had never even seen her swat a fly.

I was really missing her.

As I replanted Auntie Lisa's flowers, I wondered how Connor would have felt when Maths Club had finished and he had found his bike gone.

I thought about all the horrible things Jack would do to me the next day.

I did not want to go back to school.

I thought, what if... what if I *never* went back to school?

What would happen then?

## Chapter Eleven

## No Magic Wishes

The next day, I woke early, before Auntie Lisa. I picked up Connor's bike helmet, tucked it under one arm, and crept out of the house. I walked on my own, in the early morning half-light, down to the park gate.

On the ground, by the side of the road, was the last thing I expected to see.

Aisha's lost toy kitten was lying face down in a puddle by the gutter.

I thought about how sad Aisha had been when she lost it.

Then I thought about how mean she had been to me.

Kneeling down by the puddle, I thought about what Mum would want me to do.

Picking up Aisha's toy kitten, I pushed it into my pocket and headed into the park, over to the lake.

Not too far in, I saw Connor's bike.

It was out of my reach. Luckily, one of the nearby trees had a low-hanging branch I could hang onto, and lean over the water where one of the handlebars was just close enough for my fingertips to hook around. Tugging the bike safely out and onto the path, I noticed one side was badly scratched. At least I could return it.

It was so early, I thought nobody else would be about as I wheeled the bike back into school.

"Hey! My bike!"

My heart sank. I had thought I would able to replace Connor's bike without being seen. Out of all the people who could have been in that early, the only other person in the playground was Connor. He ran over with a beaming smile.

"You found it! Thank you. Where was it?"

I nervously shuffled my feet.

"In the lake."

It was only then Connor saw the scratches along the side.

"In the lake? What was it doing there?"

Connor's smile slowly disappeared.

"You… you didn't take my bike, did you?"

Before I could answer, I felt my face burn red in shame. Even if I'd wanted to lie, my blush was giving away the truth.

"Well… the thing is… Jack made me! I didn't want to. Now Jack says he's gonna get me! I don't know what to do. You gotta help me."

Connor wrenched his bike and helmet out of my grip.

"Help you? You must be joking! You nicked my bike!"

He did not say another word as he took his bike away.

The bell went for class.

I thought, this is it.

This was where I would have to face Jack.

No friends to help.

No ninja skills.

No magic goblin wishes.

I thought, better to see Jack in class with other people around than on my own in the playground.

As much as I did not want to be early sitting next to Connor after what had just happened, I rushed into class and did just that, to put off seeing Jack on my own for as long as I could.

## Chapter Twelve

## The Story of 'Zombie Bunny'

I sat by Connor in the worst silence ever.

In came all the other kids. Every time one came in, I cowered, expecting it to be Jack. Except Jack never came to class that morning.

Aisha did, and she gave me an angry glare before sitting down.

Everyone else from class was in except for Jack.

With Jack's usual seat empty, Miss started the lesson. She brought out from her desk a pile of papers.

"Connor," she said, "I was impressed with your imaginative story about zombie bunnies from last week's creative writing. Today, I thought we could do some acting and act out Connor's story! I have copies for anyone who would like to take part. Aisha, would you like to be a zombie bunny?"

Aisha said nothing. She seemed different today without Jack sitting beside her. I thought that this was exactly the kind of thing she would think was 'weird'; that there was no way she would ever take part. But to my surprise, Aisha *did* get up to be a zombie bunny.

Then, Miss asked Connor if he could do a zombie bunny's evil laugh.

This is the same Connor who never said anything in class to anyone. I could not believe it!

He did an evil laugh – like a crazy villain – in front of everyone, and it was brilliant.

Connor read all of his zombie bunny story at the front of class. Other children got up to make more villainous laughter and zombie bunny hops. I did not get up. I knew Connor would not want me up there with them, and I did not feel like such a monster expert any more.

With each line that he read, Connor seemed to grow in confidence.

“One night, I heard a nasty noise.
It was not a giraffe
or goat or fish or frog…
It was a zombie bunny’s laugh!

I thought, *“It’s gonna bite me!
I’ll become a zombie too!
Oh, please! Won’t someone help me?
Is there nothing I can do?”*

I tried to hide, but I was found!
So scared and drenched in sweat,
I heard the zombie bunny make
its loudest laughter yet!

And then, I heard another noise,
like someone else was near.
I heard a hero bunny give
a brilliant super cheer!

Then loads of hero bunnies
came to face this one bad guy.
I said, *“Let’s show him we’re not scared,
our cheers will fill the sky!”*

We cheered together, and that
zombie bully went away.
The day was saved and we all gave
a great *“Hip hip hooray…”* ”

The whole class joined in with loud hoorays and clapped and cheered.

This was the happiest I had seen Connor since we had met.

## Chapter Thirteen

## My Best Adventure Ever

When it was break time, I stopped Connor before he could run outside.

"I'm sorry I took your bike. I feel awful. Can I help mend it?"

Connor looked at the others, already racing about in the playground, and then looked back at me.

"No. It's OK. Everyone's scared of Jack."

"It was still my fault, I really am sorry," I said, as we walked to the playground together. "I liked your zombie bunny story."

"Yeah," smiled Connor, "but do you think anyone would've been zombie bunnies if Jack had been in?"

At that moment, some of the others from our class came over.

One of them said: "Connor, you should make up more stories."

This was the first time I had seen Connor speak to anyone else from class other than Miss or me.

"Thanks," said Connor. "My brother and me love playing zombie bunnies. If you wanted, would you like to play?"

Several children were keen. Aisha saw us and came over to join the little crowd now building around Connor. She saw what I had in my pocket.

"My kitten! Don't hurt her. Don't—"

I took the kitten out and held it towards Aisha.

"It's OK. I found her for you. Here. Would you like to play zombie bunnies?"

She looked around. I think to make certain Jack was not there.

Then, right there, in the middle of the playground, we *all* played zombie bunnies.

I will always remember this day when I made friends who are still with me now, all these years later. My friendship with them – all our games, laughter and times shared together – has been my best adventure ever.

## DOM #52/52

| **Height:** 137cm | **Eyes:** Blue |
|---|---|
| **Favourite Food:** Veggie burgers and marzipan (not combined). | |
| **Top Speed:** 100% (even on one leg due to 'Magpie' card #13 sighting). | |
| **Unique Skills:** 100% (monster expert, can memorise all stats on all 'Monster' cards). | |
| **Creativity:** 100% (rhyming stories, including incredible improvised rhymes in times of high drama and conflict). | |
| **Power Up:** Combine with 'Home-made Trophy' card #29. Former rivals share all cards (when all players share all cards, everyone wins). | |

## Chapter Fourteen

## Home

At home time, on the day we all first played zombie bunnies, Auntie Lisa was waiting for me at the school gates.

Beside her was Mum.

Mum looked much better. I gave her the biggest hug and then asked if Connor and Aisha could come back to ours.

The five of us walked down the road together, chatting about zombie bunnies and taking turns to make villainous laughter. We saw a magpie and each of us took turns to hop on one leg three times. Wonderfully weird.

However, up the road, past the park, I saw Jack. He was not alone.

Jack was outside the High School with his big brother. Jack's big brother was shoving him and Jack looked scared. Jack had another bruise on his face, even bigger than the black eye. Jack's brother stopped the shoving when he saw us getting near.

I knew Jack had seen me, but he pretended he had not.

I asked Mum what she thought was the right thing to do.

Sometimes, we do not get magic wishes to make it all better.

Sometimes, all we can do is be nice, and try to let others join in when we have fun.

Poetry and adventure for ages 5 and above.
Available from your favourite bookshops.